FIRST GRADE'S FOREVER

Written by
Robin F. Johnson

Illustrated by
Elizabeth Higgins

For Charlie Clark Johnson, who loves school as much as Wesley does.

©2017 by Robin F. Johnson
All Rights Reserved

ISBN-13: 978-1546605294   ISBN-10: 1546605290
Library of Congress Control Number: 2017909257
CreateSpace Independent Publishing Platform, North Charleston, SC

Cover art and illustrations by Elizabeth Higgins

Bearly
Tolerable
Publications

Wesley really likes spiders!
Can you find one in each of the illustrations?
Look carefully.
They might be hiding...

Wesley Briggs wasn't the smartest boy in Mr. Bottomley's first grade class. He wasn't the best at reading, or the quickest at math, or even the neatest at printing.

But Wesley Briggs really liked first grade.
He liked it a lot.

First grade was where Wesley had learned how to read. He'd stood in front of the whole class, and in a small, quiet voice he'd read a book about spiders.

"Great first try, Wesley," Mr. Bottomley had said.

And first grade was also where Wesley had learned to count past one hundred. Mr. Bottomley had told the class that there was never an end to counting.

"You can count forever and ever," Mr. Bottomley
had explained. "That's called infinity."

And finally first grade was where Wesley had written his very first story. It was a story about spiders.

Wesley really liked spiders
after he'd read the book
about them.

"This is a story to be proud of,"
Mr. Bottomley had told
Wesley, as he tacked the pages
on the Published Authors'
Wall.

So on the last day of school — a warm, sticky day in June — Wesley sat alone on the alphabet rug in the back of the room, and he was sad.

He didn't want first grade to end.
He wanted it to go on forever,
like infinity.

**Wesley knew that the other kids
didn't feel the way he did.**

Max couldn't wait for first grade to end.
He kept bouncing up and down in his seat.

"Do you have ants in your pants?"
joked Mr. Bottomley.

Gracie was the same way. She talked and talked about going camping during summer vacation.

She told the class that she would sleep in a tent, and roast marshmallows on a campfire, and catch fireflies in a glass jar.

"Leave some fireflies to light up the sky," Mr. Bottomley teased.

All his classmates laughed at this, but not Wesley.
Wesley couldn't help but notice how the classroom
had changed.

Mr. Bottomley had pulled all the posters and charts off the bulletin boards; the fiction and nonfiction books were stacked in separate piles on the table in front, and even the Turn It In Bin was empty.

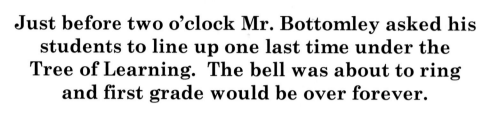

Just before two o'clock Mr. Bottomley asked his
students to line up one last time under the
Tree of Learning. The bell was about to ring
and first grade would be over forever.

Max was the first in line; Wesley was the last.

When announcements were over,
Mr. Bottomley called out in a cheery voice,
"Have a great summer vacation and a
super year in second grade!"
All the boys and girls in Mr. Bottomley's
first grade class, except for one,
hurried out the door.

Wesley just stood there, looking
down at his shoes.
"You're a little sad about leaving
first grade, aren't you, Wesley?"
asked Mr. Bottomley.
"I can understand why."

"You can?" asked Wesley in the same
small, quiet voice that he had used when
he'd read his book about spiders to the class.

"Sure I can. Do you know why we call this year first grade, Wesley?" Wesley shook his head.

"It's because in first grade you do so many things for the *first* time.

It's the *first* time you read a book all by yourself; it's the *first* time you count past one hundred, and it's the *first* time you write a story without any help," Mr. Bottomley explained.

**"No wonder you're a little sad, Wesley.
It's a very special year."**

Mr. Bottomley took Wesley's hand and walked toward the classroom door. They headed quietly down the empty hall and then outside to the bus line.

"You know, Wesley, you'll never forget this year. From now on, you'll think of first grade every time you read, or count, or write," promised Mr. Bottomley.

Wesley smiled. He liked knowing that he would remember first grade forever, maybe even for infinity.

Mr. Bottomley bent down and smiled back at Wesley. "You go home now and ask your family if they remember first grade. I bet they do."

Wesley liked that idea, too.
He turned and ran to his bus.
He wanted to catch up with Max,
who was still bouncing around
as if he had ants in his pants.

ABOUT THE AUTHOR

Robin Johnson is a former educator; during her twenty-year career, she worked with students from every grade level – kindergarten through college. She received numerous grants to enhance school libraries. Robin holds a BA from Colgate University in English and Education, an MA from Stanford University in English Literature, and advanced certification from Columbia University's Institute on the Teaching of Writing. In her spare time, she enjoys power walking, needlepoint, Scrabble, and anything that glitters! She lives with her husband in Beach Haven, NJ, and in New York City.

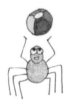

THE END

ABOUT THE ILLUSTRATOR

Elizabeth Higgins holds a BA from Bucknell University, where she studied International Relations, Spanish, and Dance. She has been drawing for as long as she can remember and loves all forms of art—from dance to painting to photography. In her spare time, Elizabeth enjoys reading books, running, and spending time outside. She lives in Boston, MA.

Made in the USA
Las Vegas, NV
21 May 2023

72368117R00021